D0979109

# *Encyclopedia Brown*

and the Case of the
Soccer Scheme

# Encyclopedia Brown
## and the Case of the Soccer Scheme

Donald J. Sobol

illustrated by James Bernardin

DUTTON CHILDREN'S BOOKS

*An imprint of Penguin Group (USA) Inc.*

DUTTON CHILDREN'S BOOKS
*A division of Penguin Young Readers Group*

Published by the Penguin Group

Penguin Group (USA) Inc., 375 Hudson Street, New York, New York 10014, U.S.A. • Penguin Group (Canada), 90 Eglinton Avenue East, Suite 700, Toronto, Ontario M4P 2Y3, Canada (a division of Pearson Penguin Canada Inc.) • Penguin Books Ltd, 80 Strand, London WC2R 0RL, England • Penguin Ireland, 25 St Stephen's Green, Dublin 2, Ireland (a division of Penguin Books Ltd) • Penguin Group (Australia), 250 Camberwell Road, Camberwell, Victoria 3124, Australia (a division of Pearson Australia Group Pty Ltd) • Penguin Books India Pvt Ltd, 11 Community Centre, Panchsheel Park, New Delhi - 110 017, India • Penguin Group (NZ), 67 Apollo Drive, Rosedale, Auckland 0632, New Zealand (a division of Pearson New Zealand Ltd) • Penguin Books (South Africa) (Pty) Ltd, 24 Sturdee Avenue, Rosebank, Johannesburg 2196, South Africa • Penguin Books Ltd, Registered Offices: 80 Strand, London WC2R 0RL, England

This book is a work of fiction. Names, characters, places, and incidents are either the product of the author's imagination or are used fictitiously, and any resemblance to actual persons, living or dead, business establishments, events, or locales is entirely coincidental.

The publisher does not have any control over and does not assume any responsibility for author or third-party websites or their content.

*Library of Congress Cataloging-in-Publication Data*
Sobol, Donald J., date.
Encyclopedia Brown and the case of the soccer scheme / by Donald J. Sobol ; illustrated by James Bernardin.—1st ed.
p. cm.—(Encyclopedia Brown)
Summary: Idaville's secret weapon against lawbreakers, ten-year-old Leroy "Encyclopedia" Brown, helps the police force solve ten new cases, the solutions to which are found in the back of the book.
ISBN 978-0-525-42582-3 (hardcover) [1. Mystery and detective stories.] I. Bernardin, James, ill. II. Title.
PZ7.S68524Epao 2012
[Fic]—dc23    2011049551

Published in the United States by Dutton Children's Books, a division of Penguin Young Readers Group, 345 Hudson Street, New York, New York 10014 • www.penguin.com/youngreaders

Designed by Jason Henry and Irene Vandervoort
Printed in USA • First Edition
10  9  8  7  6  5  4  3  2  1

*For Rose,*
*Who Deserves All the Dedications*

# CONTENTS

# *Encyclopedia Brown*

## and the Case of the Soccer Scheme

# The Case of the
# Friendly Watchdog

Idaville looked like many seaside towns on the outside. On the inside, however, Idaville was different. Very different.

No one, grown-up or child, got away with breaking the law in Idaville.

The center of the war on crime was not police headquarters. It was the redbrick house at 13 Rover Avenue. There lived Mr. and Mrs. Brown and their only child, ten-year-old Encyclopedia.

Mr. Brown was chief of police. He was

brave and smart. Whenever he came up against a case he couldn't solve, he went home to dinner.

Encyclopedia solved the case at the table. Usually by asking one question. Usually before dessert.

Chief Brown would have liked to tell everyone about Encyclopedia. Who would believe him? Who would believe that the mastermind behind Idaville's crime cleanup was a fifth grader?

So he kept his son's detective police work a secret, and so did Mrs. Brown.

Encyclopedia was content to forego fame. Helping to keep Idaville a safe place to live was the best reward.

However, he was stuck with his nickname. No one but his parents and his teachers called him by his real name, Leroy. He knew so much that everyone else called him Encyclopedia.

An encyclopedia is a book or set of

books filled with facts from *A* to *Z*. So was Encyclopedia's head. He had read more books than just about anyone in Idaville, and he never forgot what he read.

On Thursday Chief Brown was in Glenn City helping the police there solve a holdup. Right before he had left, a theft had taken place in Idaville. He had one of his officers take charge of the case, write a report, and leave a copy with Mrs. Brown.

Mrs. Brown read the report out loud. Encyclopedia listened to every word.

Jewelry was stolen Wednesday from the home of Adam and Gilda Lang. Any other watchdog would have barked at whoever committed the crime, but not their Morris. The neighbors didn't hear a sound.

Morris was a Great Dane and as friendly as a kitten. If he saw a stranger in the yard, he didn't bark. He wagged his tail.

Earlier in the year Mrs. Lang had signed him up for obedience school.

Morris could not pass the first test—sitting still for two minutes.

Mrs. Lang had urged him in no uncertain terms. "Sit, Morris, sit. For just two minutes, dear. That isn't hard. Be a love and *sit!*"

Morris decided to forget the whole thing. He dropped onto his stomach and licked his paws.

The following week Mrs. Lang entered him in Calvin's Canine College to improve his mind. He flunked.

Next she entered him in the Idaville Dog Show. Brains didn't count. Looks were all-important.

That's where Morris started disliking bald-headed men.

A woman was judging him. A trainer, who was bald as a lightbulb, tripped and knocked her down. She hurt her hip. A male judge replaced her. He, too, was bald. Morris barked like crazy at him and had to be pulled away.

Ever since then, Morris loses his temper whenever he sees a bald-headed man. He barks but never bites.

Mrs. Lang discovered her jewelry missing when she came home from a trip yesterday. Mrs. Lang's brother, Dudley Nelson, lives across the street from the Langs. The Langs were out of town for two days. Whenever they are gone, Dudley takes care of Morris.

Before they left, the Langs told Dudley to expect two repairmen in the morning. Hans was to fix the pool pump. Tex was to fix the lawn sprinklers.

Dudley tended his garden in front of his house while waiting for the two men. A little after nine o'clock Hans parked his truck by the gate of the Langs' fenced property. Two minutes later Tex drove up. Both men were bald. Neither had a hat.

Dudley told them that Morris barked at bald men. He loaned Hans a Yankee baseball cap. Hans, a baseball fan, was delighted. Dudley loaned Tex a ten-gallon Texas cowboy hat. Tex was delighted. Its wide brim shaded his face and neck.

Both men worked outside behind the house. Dudley lost sight of them. A seven-foot hedge surrounded the fence, and so the men were also out of sight of neighbors.

At ten o'clock, Hans drove off for about an hour. He returned with a bulging shopping bag. Then Tex drove off and came back in a little more than an hour. He, too, had a bulging shopping bag. When questioned by detectives, both men claimed to have gone to buy parts. That turned out to be true.

Each man was alone while the other went for parts. So each man had time to steal the jewelry. Morris never barked.

The doors to the house were locked. However, Morris goes in and out by a doggy door between the kitchen and part of the yard behind the house. It is automatically locked at five o'clock. Hans and Tex are small. Dudley said either man could have squeezed through the doggy door and into the house and stolen the jewels.

The men quit work within a minute of each other. Their tool cases could easily hold their tools and the jewels.

There the report ended.

"The report has all the facts except who was the thief, Hans or Tex," said Mrs. Brown. "It has to be one or the other."

"It's the one at whom Morris wouldn't bark," said Encyclopedia.

WAS IT TEX OR HANS?

(Turn to page 75 for the solution to "The Case of the Friendly Watchdog.")

# The Case of the
# Red Roses

Encyclopedia helped his father solve crimes all year-round. In the summer when school was out, he helped the children of the neighborhood as well. He opened a detective agency in the family garage.

After breakfast he hung out his sign:

BROWN DETECTIVE AGENCY
13 Rover Avenue
Leroy Brown, President
No case too small
25¢ per day
plus expenses

Encyclopedia used reason rather than muscle to solve cases. Once in a while, reason didn't work.

He therefore took in Sally Kimball, a classmate, as his junior partner. Sally was the best girl athlete in the school. She also had what it takes. She could tame the bullies.

On Sunday the detectives biked to the Harris Drugstore, which had the best greeting cards. Sally wanted to buy a get-well card for a friend.

Mr. Harris was at the cash register. Some thirty feet away Bugs Meany was standing at a table loaded with red roses for sale.

"What is that no-good Bugs doing by the roses?" Sally said. "He can't tell a rose from a turnip."

"He seems to be watching," Encyclopedia observed. "From the table of roses he can see the racks of candy, the line of customers waiting to pay, and Mr. Harris. I'd say Bugs is at the roses for a purpose."

Bugs Meany was the leader of a gang of tough older boys. They called themselves the Tigers. They should have called themselves the Lamp Chains. They were always pulling something shady.

Sally had dealt with Bugs and members of the Tigers many times. Last week she had taken care of a Tiger named Duke Kelly. Duke was threatening to rough up Robby Pickens unless he traded his new bicycle seat for a can of ginger ale.

Sally had told Duke to leave Robby alone.

"Go kiss your elbow," Duke had said with a sneer, and went for the first punch. He threw a left. Sally ducked and bashed his nose with a right.

Duke wobbled around like a boy looking for himself. "I must be having a bad day," he moaned, and bit the grass.

Now, ten days later, Duke, Bugs, and Robby were in Mr. Harris's drugstore. Bugs stood by the roses. Duke stood right behind Robby in the line to pay.

"I don't like this," Encyclopedia said to Sally. "Duke and Bugs are up to no good. They might be trying to get even. Robby is responsible for your punching out Duke."

As he spoke, a lady accidentally bumped her shopping cart into the table with the roses. The roses and their polished brass vases were shaken.

One of the vases toppled to the floor. The roses spilled out.

A clerk hurried over. He knelt on one knee and gathered the roses. Carefully he stuck them back in the brass vase.

By then Robby had reached the front of the line. He was paying Mr. Harris for a chocolate bar. Duke had edged nearer to Robby.

"What do I behold, Mr. Harris?" Duke suddenly thundered. "This!" He held up a chocolate bar. "I just pulled it out of Robby's back pocket!"

"That's not true," Robby exclaimed in shock.

Bugs raced from the roses to Mr. Harris. "Don't listen to the little sneak! At last he got caught. I saw him take two chocolate bars off the candy rack. He hid one in his back pocket. I saw him myself! I saw him with my own eyes!"

"Who knows how long he's been shoplifting," Duke broke in.

"We'll find out when the police work him over," Bugs said.

Mr. Harris looked uncertain. "I can't settle this at the moment, children. Wait for me out back."

Out in back Sally glared at Bugs. "You're lying, you bag of doughnuts. You didn't see

"*I was smelling the roses near the candy. Roses are the love of my life. I can smell them by the hour.*"

Robby take two chocolate bars off the candy rack and hide one."

"I saw him!" Bugs swore.

"How come you happened to see Duke lift the chocolate bar from Robby's pocket at just the right time?" Encyclopedia demanded.

"Some people are born with special gifts," Bugs boasted. He sniffed the air dreamily. "I was smelling the roses near the candy. Roses are the love of my life. I can smell them by the hour."

He sniffed twice more and gave Encyclopedia a cocksure grin. "I saw over the roses. I'm an expert on roses. Robby was at the candies. He took two chocolate bars. He slid one into his back pocket and got in line to pay for the other. It's the truth. Man, oh man! To think that I, Bugs Meany, America's teenage heartthrob, would tell a lie chokes me with unspeakable fury."

"Save the act, Bugs," Encyclopedia

said. "You and Duke tried to get Robby in trouble."

## WHAT CONVINCED ENCYCLOPEDIA?

(Turn to page 76 for the solution to "The Case of the

Red Roses.")

# The Case of the
# Jelly-Bean Holdup

On Friday Encyclopedia and Sally took the bus to Mr. Whitten's toy store where the jelly-bean contest was being held.

The boys and girls who entered the contest had to guess the number of jelly beans in a glass jar. Whoever guessed the correct number or who came closest would win the jelly beans plus a professional basketball.

The detectives were at the door of the toy store when Pete saw them.

Pistol Pete was six years old and a fan

of the Wild West. He sported a gun belt, holster, and water pistol. He drew the pistol on children who passed his house. If they didn't reach for the sky fast enough, he threatened to squirt them between the eyes. Often he made good.

His real name was Peter Peabody. The name didn't fit the fearless sheriff of Idaville, defender of law and order. So he called himself Pistol Pete.

The children of the neighborhood had another name for him. They called him the Town Bell. They often felt like wringing his neck.

He pointed his water pistol at Encyclopedia and Sally and commanded, "Stick 'em up!"

The detectives raised their hands.

"Don't shoot!" Sally said, fighting back a chuckle.

"Don't be scared. I'm just practicing my

fast draw," Pistol Pete explained. "Butch Ribrock wants me to pull a holdup at the jelly-bean contest."

Everyone got along with Butch Ribrock by keeping their distance. He looked like he had his fun knocking out a Ford with a smack on the bumper.

"Butch promised me I'd get my name in the newspapers if I held up the jelly-bean contest," Pistol Pete said. "I'll be the most famous gunslinger west of California."

"I think we'd better keep an eye on Butch," Encyclopedia said.

"Every minute," Sally agreed.

"Butch is sure he'll win the contest," Pistol Pete stated. "He promised me half the jelly beans."

"You told him you'd pull the holdup?" Encyclopedia asked in amazement.

"Sure," replied Pistol Pete. "I'll just be doing my thing." He twirled his water pistol into his holster like a pro.

"Butch fast-talked you," Sally said. "Don't pull a holdup half-cocked. Think it over first."

The small gunslinger was thinking it over as the detectives entered the toy store. A crowd of children was waiting for the jelly-bean contest to begin.

Mr. Whitten, the owner of the toy store, came from a back room. He carried a glass jar full of jelly beans. With him was his niece, Trudy Pickens.

Instantly Encyclopedia was alerted. Trudy had a crush on Butch Ribrock.

Mr. Whitten put the jar of jelly beans on top of a counter. He wrote on a card and showed it to Trudy. Then he slid the card under the jar.

"I've written the winning number of jelly beans on the card," he announced. "Only Trudy and I know the number."

Trudy passed out paper and pencils. The children were to write down the number of jelly beans they thought were in the jar.

Suddenly a high-pitched voice demanded, "Stick 'em up!"

It was Pistol Pete. He was pointing his gun at Trudy.

Trudy seemed nervous. She held up five fingers on her left hand and only four on her right. Her right thumb was bent into her palm.

"Why the bent thumb?" Sally whispered to Encyclopedia.

"Don't know yet," Encyclopedia whispered back.

"The jelly beans or your life," Pistol Pete snarled.

"Get lost!" someone cried. "Who opened your cage?" someone else cried. Those were the kindest remarks.

"Uh-oh," the shortest sheriff in America muttered. "Time to hit the trail." He squirted himself in the head and went thataway out the door.

Trudy collected the papers and pencils

and passed them to Mr. Whitten. He read out loud the number of jelly beans the children had written.

"I'm sorry," he said. "No one has it right so far. But forty-five is closest." He glanced over the children. "Do I have everyone's number?"

"Not mine," shouted Butch as he scribbled on his paper. He passed it to Mr. Whitten.

Mr. Whitten raised Butch's paper and the card from under the jelly-bean jar. On both was written 54.

"Fifty-four is correct!" Mr. Whitten announced. "We have a winner!"

"How could Butch guess the winning number?" Sally wondered. "He had to cheat!"

"I'm sure he did," Encyclopedia said.

WHAT MADE ENCYCLOPEDIA SURE?

(Turn to page 77 for the solution to "The Case of the Jelly-Bean Holdup.")

# The Case of the
# Soccer Scheme

On the field in South Park the Chipmunks and Cobras soccer teams were warming up for the game to decide the league championship for boys twelve and under.

Encyclopedia and Sally stood on the sideline with Hugh Canfield, a school friend. Hugh was manager of the Chipmunks.

"Who are those two Cobras?" Sally asked. "The ones heading the ball to each other."

"They're the Hackanstack twins, Vince and Vernon," Hugh said.

"They look awful tough," Sally said.

"They're mean and tough," Hugh replied. "They talk trash to the other team. They say things like, 'With a head like yours, you can be sure of one point.'"

"How can you tell which twin is which?" Sally said. "Jerseys ought to have more than a number. They should have the player's name, too. The Cobra uniforms have just numbers."

"That wouldn't help because they have the same last name," Hugh said. "A soccer uniform usually has just a number."

The game started and wasn't three minutes old when the referee blew his whistle.

"Chipmunk number eight, you were holding," he called.

He awarded the Cobras a free kick from the spot of the foul. The spot was too far from the Chipmunks' goal to threaten a score.

"It looked to me like the Cobra did the holding," Sally said.

A woman near Sally turned and spoke sharply. "The referee calls them as he sees them. He's closer to the action than you are. You should learn to respect authority, young lady."

"Must be a Cobra mother," Hugh mumbled.

Five minutes later, the referee called a foul against a Cobra. "You were holding, Bob," he said. "Because number eight of the Chipmunks held you earlier, don't try to get even. I want a clean game."

A Chipmunk kicked downfield. A Cobra player trapped the ball and back-footed it to a teammate. A Chipmunk player cut off the pass and stole the ball.

"Attaboy, Frank!" Hugh hollered at the Chipmunk.

Frank sparked an attack that kept the ball deep in the Cobras' end of the field.

The Cobras defended well. The Chipmunks failed to score.

The half ended in a 0–0 deadlock.

Late in the second half the referee blew his whistle and pointed to a Chipmunk. "Number three," he hollered, "you were charging."

"That's Rick Haywood," Hugh said. "Cool it, Rick!"

Rick had let loose a landslide of protests. The referee waved a yellow card at him.

"A warning," Hugh said anxiously. "If Rick doesn't calm down, it's good-bye. He's out of the game! Our one substitute banged up his foot skateboarding. If Rick gets thrown out, we'll be ten men against the Cobras' eleven."

Rick didn't calm down. He pinched his nose and stomped around. The referee warned him again and finally waved him out of the game.

Play went on. The Chipmunks held off

the Cobras' attacks despite having one less player and an overdose of the Hackanstack twins.

The twins played by their own rules. In front of the referee they were as well mannered as boys at a garden party. Behind the referee's back they acted like a demolition derby. They grabbed jerseys, dug elbows into ribs, tripped, and charged.

The Chipmunk rooters screamed. The referee was unmoved. He was watching the player with the ball. He couldn't call a foul he did not see.

"There are seventeen rules in soccer, and the twins have broken all of them this season," Hugh said.

With fewer than two minutes to play, a Cobra fell in the close-quarter battling by the Chipmunk goal. He lay on the ground as if in terrible pain.

The referee immediately blew his whistle.

"Chipmunk number four, you pushed Vince off the ball," he said.

Maybe, Encyclopedia thought. The push wasn't clear from the sideline.

The referee stooped over to the fallen Cobra, one of the Hackanstack twins. "Are you all right, Vince?"

"I'll be all right," Vince said bravely.

The pushing had been called within the penalty zone. The referee awarded the Cobras a penalty kick.

The players on both teams took positions ten feet from where the referee had placed the ball on the ground. Unlike a free kick, a penalty kick could be stopped only by the goalie.

Vince, who had suddenly become unhurt, strode to the ball. He had a clear, straight, 12-yard shot to the goal. Art Drum, the Chipmunk goalie, crouched, ready to spring for the ball.

"Art has to be lucky," Hugh said glumly. "A goalie seldom stops a penalty kick."

The braces on Vince's teeth flashed in a wicked grin as he stepped up and kicked. The ball flew past Art and into the net.

The Cobras' rooters cheered and slapped each other on the back.

With one fewer player, the Chipmunks couldn't break through the Cobras' defense before time ran out.

The Cobras won, 1–0.

"The game shouldn't count," Sally grumbled. "The referee helped the Cobras win. How can we prove it, Encyclopedia?"

"Easily," replied the boy detective. "The referee said so."

## WHAT DID THE REFEREE SAY?

(Turn to page 78 for the solution to "The Case of the Soccer Scheme.")

# The Case of the
# Hole in the Book

Raindrops danced on the roof of the Brown
Detective Agency.

"We may as well quit for the day," Sally
said. "Nobody will come in this weather."

"How about going to the public library?"
Encyclopedia suggested. "I can loan you a
raincoat and hat."

"Suits me," Sally said.

The two detectives made it to the library
somewhat drier than wetter.

Ms. Moore, the head librarian, came

around her desk. "How nice to see you both," she said.

"It's good to be here," Encyclopedia said. "Have you any new books?"

"Not since you were here last," replied Ms. Moore. "In fact, we have one less book. Harry Elton's novel *Fast Wheels* had a hole burned into the middle pages. It's ruined."

"When was the hole discovered?" Encyclopedia asked.

"Three nights ago," Ms. Moore said. "Ben Considine, who cleans after hours, found it in the restroom. The book was by the sink. He said the book smelled slightly of tobacco. When he opened it, he saw the hole."

"Do you suspect Ben?" asked Sally.

Ms. Moore shook her head. "Ben has been with us for years. The hole was clearly made by a cigarette being snuffed out. Ben doesn't smoke."

"Have you any idea who did it?" Encyclopedia inquired.

"I'd have to guess," Ms. Moore answered. "It rained that day, worse than today. No one came into the library except four teenage boys. They use the library once in a while. They checked out books on racing cars and drivers. They stayed about thirty minutes. I think it was one of them."

Ms. Moore showed the detectives the burned book. "What sort of person would do such a thing?" she said bitterly.

Encyclopedia examined the hole.

"Does it tell you anything?" Sally asked hopefully.

"Not so far," the boy detective said. "Do you have the boys' names, Ms. Moore?"

"I can get their names off their library cards," Ms. Moore said.

She used the computer and showed the printout to the detectives. On it were four names: Chris Wilder, Oscar Lane, Gary Silver, and Frank Cloud.

The detectives had seen them in town. They were not troublemakers.

"Did anything unusual happen in the library since the hole was made?" Encyclopedia asked.

"I can't say," Ms. Moore replied. "While the boys were here, my two assistants, Ms. Catlin and Ms. Hawkins, were in the office. They were checking in books returned in the book drop. None of us watched the boys. Wait, there is something else."

She drew a folded sheet of paper from her desk drawer. "I received this in the mail today."

The top two lines on the sheet were:

He burned the hole in the book.

To find out who, have a look.

Written below in block letters were three words, PURPLE MONTH ORANGE.

"I can't see that the three words have anything to do with the burned hole. They don't make sense," said Ms. Moore. "I think it's an attempt to throw us off the track."

"Perhaps it's a code," Sally said.

"Possibly," Encyclopedia said.

"Month," Ms. Moore mused. "Months have holidays. Is there a holiday with purple and orange colors? Then again, the code may have to do with food. Grape jelly is purple, and oranges are orange. The words may be about a holiday or food."

"Are there any holidays about food, Encyclopedia?" Sally asked.

"I only know of two, Picnic Day in Australia and Peanut Sunday in Luxembourg," Encyclopedia said.

"Australia? Luxembourg? Good grief, that's reaching a little too far, isn't it?" Ms.

*"I can't see that the three words have anything to do with the
burned hole. They don't make sense," said Ms. Moore.*

Moore objected politely. "The code may have to do with poetry some way or other. Rhyming book with look may be a clue."

"That's it!" Encyclopedia exclaimed. "The words purple, orange, and month don't tell us who wrote them. They tell us who burned the hole in the book."

## WHO BURNED THE HOLE?

(Turn to page 79 for the solution to "The Case of the Hole in the Book.")

# The Case of the
# April Fools' Plot

Every morning Chuck Tweedle delivered the *Idaville News* around the neighborhood on his bike. He slung the newspaper to the front doors with great skill.

In the week since April Fools', however, the newspaper landed several feet from the doors. One homeowner, Mr. Miller, complained the loudest, but only about the delivery on April Fools'.

Encyclopedia and Sally decided to learn more from Chuck himself. The detectives found him sitting on the front steps of his house huddled in gloom.

Sally laid her hand gently on his shoulder. "Gosh, Chuck, whatever is the matter?"

"I was fired," Chuck said.

"What for?" Encyclopedia asked. "You deliver the newspaper on time, and your aim is perfect—right to the front door."

"I never missed," Chuck said. "How else can a half-pint like me make a name for himself?"

"You're already a name," Sally said. "You became one last year when you were crowned the *Idaville News* delivery boy of the year."

"That dumps me into a class with last year's news," Chuck replied. "I didn't deserve to be fired. I didn't do what I'm supposed to have done."

"Tell us," Encyclopedia said.

"What have I got left to lose?" Chuck said halfheartedly.

"On April Fools'," he began, "I delivered the newspaper to the Millers' house by six thirty, as always. That afternoon Mr. Miller complained that I had rolled up the newspaper. When it was tight and hard, he said I shoved it though the handle of the front door, bolting the door shut."

"Did you?" Encyclopedia asked.

"I didn't do any such thing," Chuck said. "My boss said I couldn't work for the *Idaville News* after such a trick, April Fools' or not. He said to pick up my check and have a nice day."

"Anyone could have bolted the door after you delivered the newspaper to the Millers," Encyclopedia said.

"Did anyone see you deliver the newspaper to the Millers?" Sally asked.

"Mr. Miller's teenage daughter, Lily," Chuck answered. "She's a singer and a cat lover. She has three white cats, beautiful but a mess. They leave hairs wherever they lie down. They sleep nights in the living room on the couch facing the picture window. When I tossed the paper at her door on April Fools', I saw the cats lying on the couch. Lily claims she saw me bolt the door. I didn't see her. She wasn't on the couch."

"Why should she lie?" Sally said.

"To help her kid brother, Horace," Chuck replied. "I beat him out for the newspaper delivery route. He wanted it. He's got it now."

"Let's hear from Lily," Encyclopedia said.

Lily wasn't pleased to see them. She took them into the living room. "Have a seat," she said coldly.

On the way to a chair, Encyclopedia stopped behind the couch. It bore a mess of white cats' hair.

The living room was in the wing of the

house. The picture window allowed him to see the front door. Cats' hair or no cats' hair, the couch was plainly the best place to see all of the door.

"What's on your mind, such as it is?" Lily inquired.

"You said you saw Chuck bolt your front door with a newspaper on April Fools'," Encyclopedia said. "Could you be mistaken?"

"Not on your life," Lily hurled back. "It was Chuck."

"Chuck said he delivered the newspaper at your house by six thirty. You had to be up early," Sally declared.

"I never sleep well before I have to perform," Lily said. "I had to perform at a charity breakfast at the Children's Hospital that morning. The breakfast included dancing to the music of the six-piece band, the Black Ties. I'm their singer."

"Dancing at breakfast?" said Sally.

"It's never too early to dance," Lily retorted. "The program started at nine o'clock. All of us, musicians, waiters, and cooks, had to report at eight to set things up. I got up a little after five."

"What did you do with all that time to kill, from five to eight?" Sally puzzled.

"I decided to get ready and wait for the newspaper," Lily said impatiently. "So I freshened up and put on the black linen dress I always wear when singing with the Black Ties. I thought I'd read the newspaper while I had breakfast."

"Weren't you worried about soiling your dress at breakfast?" Sally asked. "If I had to perform, I wouldn't dress up until I'd eaten."

"My black dress is always spotless. I take care of all my clothes," Lily snapped. "I'm not ten years old."

"Where were you when Chuck delivered the newspaper?" said Encyclopedia.

Lily rolled her eyes. "Where would I be able to see Chuck at the front door? I was sitting on the couch!"

Sally howled. "You sat on the cats?"

Lily laughed scornfully. "Don't be silly, you twit. I chased them off first."

All at once she stopped laughing. Her face looked as if she'd been hit over the head with the floor.

Encyclopedia had told her how he knew she was not telling the truth.

HOW DID ENCYLOPEDIA KNOW?

(Turn to page 80 for the solution to "The Case of the April Fools' Plot.")

# The Case of
# Wilford's Big Deal

Danny Proxmire, who was eight, laid twenty-five cents on the empty gas can by Encyclopedia. "I'm hiring you."

"For what?" asked Encyclopedia.

"Wilford Wiggins called a secret meeting for little kids at five o'clock. He promised to make us rich beyond imagining," Danny said.

"Wilford, oh that Wilford!" Sally groaned. *"Phew!"*

Wilford Wiggins was a high-school dropout and as peppy as seaweed washed up on the beach. He swore he wasn't afraid of work. He had fought it for years.

"The only exercise he gets is yawning," Sally said.

Wilford championed the grand old rule. Never stand if you can sit and never sit if you can lie down. While on his back he dreamed up new ways to cheat the little kids out of their piggy-bank savings.

Last month he was raising money to save the Pony Express. A week ago it was funds for an electric napkin. It lit up so you could see to wipe your mouth in the dark.

Wilford never got away with his phony get-rich deals, however. Encyclopedia was always there to stop him.

"You can't trust Wilford," Sally advised Danny.

"That's why I'm here," Danny said. "I need you to make sure he's on the up-and-up this time."

"Wilford wouldn't be on the up-and-up in a ski lift," Sally said.

"We'll take the case," Encyclopedia said.

Wilford usually held his secret meetings in the city dump. This one was in the dance classroom of the Community Center.

"The dance class for today was called off," Danny said to the detectives. "The teacher had to fly to Akron. Wilford gets to use the room because he claimed his talk is educational. It teaches little kids how to invest their money wisely. Lucky for us, this secret meeting isn't in the city dump again. We won't go home stinky."

The dance classroom at the Community Center was overcrowded with little kids eager to hear Wilford on how to get rich quick.

Wilford was standing in front of the children, about to offer them his newest can't-lose moneymaking deal. Beside him stood a thin, pale-faced teenager holding a knapsack.

"Meet Bruno McCumber," Wilford announced in the voice of a duke introducing the king of England.

Bruno bent in a modest bow. Encyclopedia remembered seeing him around town.

He was usually admiring himself in the nearest mirror.

"Bruno got home yesterday from the desert where he'd been for three months prospecting for gold," Wilford said. "He barely had enough water to stay alive. It was hot and rainless. But Bruno, alone day and night, didn't give up. Thirsty and tired, he kept digging. Finally he struck pay dirt, and here it is. Show 'em, Bruno!"

Bruno carefully shook a few bright yellow pebbles from his knapsack. He held them for everyone to see.

"Yeah, yeah, yeah," a boy cried. "Cut

the lip drip and get to it." Other children joined in, demanding Wilford get to his new moneymaking deal.

"Those are no ordinary pebbles you see," Wilford sang. "That's gold! Bruno discovered the richest gold mine in the state."

The children gasped.

"Men who dig for gold keep their finds a secret," a boy challenged. "How come you're telling us?"

"Glad you asked, friend," Wilford said. "You don't use a pick and shovel to mine gold today. Too slow. We must have modern machinery. I'll be honest with you. All our cash is tied up in African oil wells. So I thought of selling shares to my little pals in Idaville. Help us buy the machinery, and Bruno and I will make you rich beyond imagining."

"Don't leak a word about the mine,"

*"Those are no ordinary pebbles you see," Wilford sang. "That's gold! Bruno discovered the richest gold mine in the state."*

Bruno counseled. "If you do, the grown-ups will move in and grab it all. None of us will get a dime."

"And your dreams won't come true," Wilford added. "You won't be able to buy things for your mom and dad, like a new car or a washing machine."

"How much is a share?" a girl hollered.

"The regular price is twenty dollars," Wilford said. "For my little pals, I'll tell you what I'm going to do. I'll slash the price to two dollars a share. In three years a share will be worth a fortune! The more shares you buy, the sooner you can buy that car or washing machine for your mom and dad."

The children chattered excitedly. How long would it take to afford a new car or a washing machine if they bought ten or twenty shares?

Wilford had them set up for his best line: "Don't blame me that you're poor. Blame me for making you rich."

That did it. The children lined up to buy shares.

"Stop them, Encyclopedia," Sally pleaded. "Don't let Wilford walk off with their savings."

"I won't," Encyclopedia assured her. "There is no gold mine."

WHY DID ENCYCLOPEDIA SAY THAT?

(Turn to page 81 for the solution to "The Case of Wilford's Big Deal.")

# The Case of the
# Ten-Dollar Bike

Nine-year-old Mitzi Bowser dragged herself into the Brown Detective Agency.

"Am I a blockhead?" she groaned, and laid a quarter on the gas can. "Yesterday Agatha Grubs talked me into secretly buying a like-new bicycle from her for ten dollars. She said she needed money badly. I paid her five dollars to hold the bike for me, even though I haven't seen it yet."

"You should have been warned about Agatha," Sally said. "The less you have to do with her the better off you'll be."

Agatha Grubs was twelve, and walked with a heavy step. Little kids got out of her way.

"I wonder what kind of a bike she's selling," Encyclopedia said.

"Let me guess," Sally put in. "Agatha said that the wheels hum 'Happy Days Are Here Again'?"

Mitzi smiled weakly. "Naw, but Agatha said I'll love the bike the minute I see it. She promised to hold it for me until noon today. She won't sell it to someone else before then."

Mitzi brooded briefly.

"Agatha knows I need a bike," she continued. "If I don't pay her the rest of the money when I see it, she'll keep the five dollars for her trouble. Did I get taken!"

"We've got an hour till the noon deadline," Encyclopedia said. "A visit to the bike is in order."

Agatha's house was three blocks away. She welcomed Mitzi. She fixed the detectives with a look that said, "May a cow fall on your head."

"We're here to see your ten-dollar bike," Sally announced.

"The bike is none of your business," Agatha said coldly.

"I asked them to come," Mitzi said.

"I said you see the bike alone or the sale is off," Agatha said, "and I keep the five dollars."

"I forgot," Mitzi said meekly.

"I have nothing more to say," Agatha growled, "and I'm only going to say it once."

Sally clenched her fists. "Show us the bike."

"Buzz off," Agatha said.

"We better leave," Encyclopedia told Sally.

If it came to a showdown, Encyclopedia had no doubt Sally would jab Agatha dizzy. Still, Agatha was no pushover, being built somewhat along the lines of a truck stop.

The detectives crossed the street. Shielded by a passing car, they ducked behind two empty garbage pails standing at the curb. From there they could see what went on between Agatha and Mitzi.

Agatha brought from her garage a shiny blue two-wheel bicycle.

"That must be the bike Agatha's selling," Sally said. "Agatha's mom told my mom about it in the supermarket. It has everything. A basket, lights, water bottle, and a tire pump."

From behind the garbage cans the detectives saw Agatha climb on the bike and nothing more. A city truck parked in front of them, blocking their view.

"Bad luck," Encyclopedia said. "If we move and Agatha sees us watching, she'll call off the sale. She'll have an excuse to keep the bike and Mitzi's five dollars."

The detectives could do nothing but wait.

After a few minutes, they peeked. It was

safe. The demonstration was over. They stepped around the truck. They reached Mitzi as Agatha was walking the bike back into the garage.

"It's a beautiful bike," Sally said to Mitzi.

"Yeah," said Mitzi, "except for the pedals."

"I don't understand," Sally said.

Mitzi explained. "When the pedal on the left goes forward, the one on the right goes backward—and vice versa. That bike is dangerous! The pedals don't turn the same way."

Agatha had come from of the garage. "I heard what you said, Mitzi. Yesterday I told you straight out the pedals were damaged. If you buy it, you'll have to bring it to a bicycle shop and have the pedals fixed. I don't know how much it will cost—probably not more than fifty or sixty dollars."

"You told me I could fix the pedals myself!" Mitzi yelped. "Now you tell me it might cost fifty or sixty dollars to fix. I don't think I can buy the bike."

"Fine with me," Agatha said. "As we agreed, I keep your five dollars if you don't buy the bike."

"Not hardly," Encyclopedia said.

## WHY NOT?

(Turn to page 82 for the solution to "The Case of the Ten-Dollar Bike.")

## The Case of the
## Hidden Money

"That was Lou Warwick on the phone," Chief Brown said. "I better get right over. A lot of money was stolen from his desk today."

Lou was a retired Army veteran. He had become bored with fishing and golfing and muddling around the house. For the past thirteen years he had fixed up old military vehicles for fun and sometimes for profit.

"Why not take Leroy along?" Mrs. Brown said. "He's always helped you."

"How about it, Leroy? Want to come?" Chief Brown said.

"Do I!" exclaimed Encyclopedia. Going with his father on a police case was the treat of treats.

Lou was in his specially built garage. It was big enough to house Jeeps, armored cars, a field ambulance, and a Sherman tank. He hailed Chief Brown and Encyclopedia from atop the tank.

"Wherever did you find it?" Chief Brown said, marveling at the huge machine.

"At an auction six months ago," Lou replied. "I had to have it. My wife thought I belonged in a cuckoo nest. We traded off. She could continue collecting Peruvian hairless cats. I could keep the tank."

He rapped the tank with the side of his fist. "Moving, it sounds like a train wreck, but it'll do twenty-five miles an hour going downhill."

He hopped to the ground, his expression suddenly serious.

"The money was stolen from my office," he said. "I thought I could solve the theft myself. I can't. I don't want to accuse anyone without being sure."

"Over the phone you said the money was stolen from your desk. Let's have a look," Chief Brown said.

Lou led them into his office.

"The door from the garage to the office is locked only when the day's work is done," Lou said. "The door on the other wall opens to the house. It's also locked after work."

Besides a desk and chair the office had bookshelves, a four-drawer filing cabinet, a watercooler, and a bathroom.

"Did any stranger enter your office today?" Chief Brown asked.

"This morning a couple from St. Paul bought an amphibious Jeep to use for exploring and camping," Lou said. "They paid cash—with hundred-dollar bills and some twenties and fifties. They brought the money in a knapsack. They took the knapsack with them."

He paused, arranging the details of the crime in his memory.

"I've always been paid by check," he resumed. "I had only large manila envelopes in which to carry the cash to the bank. I had shoved in most of the bills when I was called to attend to a customer. I hurried to the garage, leaving the envelopes on my desk. For thirty minutes I was tied up with the customer—a waste. He was just looking. When I got back to the office, the envelopes and the money were gone."

"While you were with the customer, did you notice anyone go in and out of the office?" Chief Brown inquired.

"Yes, all three of my staff did," Lou said. "First Ed Winslow, then Phil Riggs, then Olga Simpson. They swore they had nothing to do with the theft. I have to believe them.

The envelopes are too big to smuggle away unnoticed. The bills are too many to be hidden in the thief's clothes. I want you to hear what each has to say, Chief. I may have overlooked something."

Ed Winslow, the mechanic, had been the first to enter the office. He told Chief Brown, "I had a drink at the watercooler. The manila envelopes were on Lou's desk with a few bills sticking out. I didn't touch them."

Phil Riggs, who did the body work, was the second to enter the office. He told Chief Brown that after Ed left it, he too had gone for a drink at the watercooler. "The manila envelopes were on the desk," he said. "I saw a few bills. I didn't steal anything."

Olga Simpson, the last one to go into the office, was a small, white-haired woman. She handled the paperwork. She told Chief Brown she had been in the office to have a drink at the watercooler after Phil. She saw the envelopes and a few bills on the desk. "I left them there," she insisted.

Lou shut the office door after her and sank into the desk chair.

"The thief could have jimmied the locked front door, slipped into the office from the house, stolen the money, and got out the same way," he said. "But my wife is at home. She would have called out if she heard someone in the house."

Encyclopedia didn't need to hear more. "May I say something, Dad?" he asked.

"Certainly," Chief Brown replied.

"The money is still in the office," Encyclopedia said.

"That doesn't make sense!" objected Lou. "I've searched every inch—the cabinet drawers, the desk drawers, the bookshelves, the bathroom, the watercooler stand, everywhere."

"Not quite everywhere," Encyclopedia said. "The money is hidden where no one would think of looking—under the filing cabinet. Olga is the thief. She plans to come back for the money in her own good time."

"The filing cabinet is full and weighs too much for anyone to lift," Lou said. "How can she be the thief?"

"She counted on your believing she can't," Encyclopedia said.

## HOW DID OLGA HIDE THE MONEY?

(Turn to page 83 for the solution to "The Case of the

Hidden Money.")

# The Case of
# Lovely Lana

Every year the Idaville Pet Fish Club held its show in Mrs. Finley's backyard. This year the show fell on a day Encyclopedia visited his grandmother.

Sally attended the Pet Fish Club Show alone. Her friend Ginger Butterworth had entered a fish. Sally didn't want to hurt Ginger's feelings by staying away. In her opinion staring at fish was best done during a few moments of spare time.

She was to learn pet fish could scale the heights of a mystery.

At the show she saw Ginger was standing by a row of small show tanks set on a bench. Each tank contained a tiny fish.

"Meet my Lovely Lana," Ginger said in greeting Sally. She tapped the tank containing a fish two inches long. "Isn't she beautiful? She's a killifish."

"She doesn't move," Sally said. "Is she sick?"

"No, that's a good sign, according to Earl Duffy. She'll do well in the judging. She's not stressed out like this one." Ginger indicated the fish cringing on the bottom of the next tank.

"Wherever did you learn about pet fish?" Sally asked.

"Earl Duffy taught me," Ginger said. "He told me what to feed her and how to care for her. He insists I give her Canadian earthworms, which are fat and juicy. Food can make or break a champion, Earl says."

Ginger related how she came to own

"*Meet my Lovely Lana,*" *Ginger said in greeting Sally. She tapped the tank containing a fish two inches long. "Isn't she beautiful? She's a killifish.*"

Lovely Lana. She had been strolling through a farmer's market when she noticed a counter loaded with tanks of small pet fish. Half an hour later she passed the counter again. All the fish but one had been sold.

"I nearly forgot to display this one," the woman at the counter had said. "It's a newborn."

Earl Duffy, a ninth grader, had stopped to watch.

"That's a mighty fine killifish," he had said to Ginger. "Buy it. I'd buy it myself except I spent all my cash already. Besides, I have a killifish named Prince. I had two other killifish. They were born the same day, lived a long time, and died on the same day. It was sad."

He tapped his temples. "I was a beginner and dumb. I left the lid closed on their tank too long, cutting off air. But I studied up. Prince is in shape to win Best in Show at the Pet Fish Club Show this year."

Ginger cooed at her killifish. "On Earl's advice," she said to Sally, "I bought the killifish and named it Lovely Lana. I told Earl I was going to enter her in the Pet Fish Club Show. At home I put her in a soup bowl before Earl loaned me a handsome glass vase for her. The bottom was a bowl. It rose in a long narrow neck to a small opening at the top. Earl explained the vase was meant for a single flower, but right for a killifish."

"Why is that?" Sally asked.

"Earl said the small opening at the top of the vase will keep Lovely Lana from jumping out," Ginger answered. "Killifish are pet fish and were known to jump in the air the instant a lid was lifted, killing themselves."

Ginger paused to coo again at Lovely Lana which floated like a log. "Am I lucky," she said. "Oops, Mrs. Finley has started."

Mrs. Finley had stepped to the fish tanks. She began the judging.

"Pet fish are a hobby," Ginger said in a low voice. "This isn't about fame and big bucks like a dog show. You can hold and feel dogs. There really isn't much you can do with a fish. They don't sit or roll over. They swim or they don't."

Mrs. Finley inspected the fish with a trained eye. She spoke of the good or bad points of each fish. "Sunken belly, sign of bad health." "Humpback, too old." "Stressed out," and so on.

An assistant wrote her remarks on an official judging sheet.

Mrs. Finley reached Earl's killifish, Prince. She seemed pleased by what she saw.

"If I don't win, I hope Earl does," Ginger said.

Mrs. Finley judged two more fish before coming to Lovely Lana. "Hmmm," she murmured. She shook the vase gently. Lovely Lana bobbed in place. "Hmmm," she repeated.

When she had studied all the fish, the assistant handed her the judging sheet. Mrs. Finley read it silently and then announced, "Best in Show, Ginger Butterworth's killifish!"

She presented Ginger with the blue ribbon and a fifteen-dollar gift certificate to the Fish and Nip pet shop.

Earl leaped like a kangaroo. "I can't believe you chose that fish!" he gasped.

"Why not, Earl?" Mrs. Finley questioned.

"Because it's dead, that's why not!" Earl wailed. "Anyone can see it's dead. Dead is *dead*!"

"But Earl, it has perfect fins and shows well," Mrs. Finley said. "It's just dead."

"This is crazy!" Earl blurted. "*Crazy!*"

Mrs. Finley dealt with him calmly.

"Many years ago in Medina, Ohio," she said, "one fish died sometime after it arrived at the show but before the judging. It won

Best in Show and fathered a rule almost forgotten. A fish that dies after arrival at a show can still compete. All the fish were checked when they arrived for the show today. Ginger's killifish was alive."

"You tried to keep Lovely Lana out of the show, Earl," Sally said, "but you goofed."

## HOW HAD EARL TRIED?

(Turn to page 84 for the solution to "The Case of

Lovely Lana.")

Solution to **The Case of the Friendly Watchdog**

Tex couldn't be the thief. In order to squeeze through the doggy door and into the house, he would have had to take off his wide-brimmed ten-gallon hat. Morris would have barked at his bald head. But no barking was heard.

The thief was Hans, who wore a baseball cap. He didn't have to take it off and show his bald head. He could squeeze through the doggy door without a worry about losing the cap and making Morris bark.

Solution to **The Case of the Red Roses**

Bugs insisted he saw Duke lift a candy bar from Robby's pocket. Bugs said he saw everything while smelling the roses.

Impossible! The vase that toppled to the floor spilled out roses but no water. The clerk proved the floor was dry. He would never have knelt on a wet floor. Flowers in a vase without water are artificial. Artificial flowers have no smell!

To make sure the roses hadn't been given a scent, as sometimes they do, Encyclopedia sniffed them. His wink at Sally told her the flowers had no scent.

Mr. Harris let Bugs and Duke off when they bought Robby both candy bars.

Solution to **The Case of the Jelly-Bean Holdup**

When Pistol Pete told her to raise her hands, Trudy was to signal Butch Ribrock with her fingers the number of jelly beans in the jar.

Trudy was nervous. She showed five fingers on her left hand and only four on her right because of the bent thumb. She thought she was telling Butch 54.

But she read 54 from *her* side. The fingers facing the children read 45.

When Mr. Whitten said the closest number was 45, Butch understood Trudy's error. He scribbled 54.

When Mr. Whitten heard that from Encyclopedia, he awarded the jelly beans and basketball to Gaylord Hallstrom, the one who guessed 45.

Solution to ***The Case of the Soccer Scheme***

The referee's calls weren't honest mistakes, Encyclopedia realized. The calls favored the Cobras. The referee did not know the Chipmunk players. He had to call them by their numbers. He sided with the Cobra players because he knew them well. He called them by their names.

The president of the soccer league heard what Encyclopedia had to say about the referee. The game was played over with another referee. The Chipmunks won, 3–2.

Solution to ***The Case of the
Hole in the Book***

When Ms. Moore said "rhyme," Encyclopedia understood the code. He remembered purple, orange, and month are three of the four words that lack a rhyme. The fourth word, silver, named the guilty boy—Gary Silver.

Gary admitted to his pals he had sneaked into the restroom for a smoke and took the book with him. Thinking someone was coming in, he quickly snuffed out the cigarette in the book. He hid the cigarette in his pocket.

One of his pals believed Gary should not get away with ruining the book. Rather than be a snitch, the pal wrote the code. Let someone else figure out the thief.

Gary had to pay for the book he ruined.

"One more reason not to smoke," remarked Encyclopedia.

Solution to ***The Case of the
April Fools' Plot***

Lily lied about seeing Chuck bolt the front door while she sat on the couch. Although the couch was the best place from which to see the front door, Lily would never sit down where white cats had slept. She would not want their white cat hair soiling her black dress that she wore when singing with the Black Ties band.

She had framed Chuck in order for her brother, Horace, to take over the newspaper route. Thanks to Encyclopedia, Chuck got it back.

Solution to **The Case of Wilford's Big Deal**

Wilford claimed Bruno had just gotten back from three months of prospecting in the desert for gold. The desert was hot and rainless, Wilford said.

Encyclopedia realized the bright yellow pebbles weren't bits of gold but merely pebbles painted yellow. Bruno couldn't have found them in the desert as he claimed.

Being in the desert sun for three months would have given him a mean sunburn.

His face, however, was pale.

Solution to **The Case of the Ten-Dollar Bike**

Agatha never meant to sell the bike. She wanted to keep the five dollars that Mitzi gave her. She tried to get Mitzi to call off the sale by tricking her into thinking something was wrong with the bike.

There was nothing wrong with the pedals, Encyclopedia said.

Mitzi was looking at the left side of the bike while Agatha rode it. From this view, when the left pedal moved forward, the pedal on the right moved backward. Pedaling moves the chain connected to the back wheel, which makes the wheel turn and the bike move forward. Mitzi was so confused by Agatha, that the pedals turning this way only *seemed* wrong to her.

Agatha had to sell the bike to Mitzi for only ten dollars, as she had agreed.

Solution to ***The Case of the
Hidden Money***

Olga made the mistake of saying the envelopes were
on the desk when she went for a drink. She obviously
didn't know she was the last one in the office.
Unwittingly she cleared Ed Winslow and Phil Riggs.

Encyclopedia showed how she hid the money.
He pulled out each filing cabinet drawer until it was
stopped by a latch. The cabinet was now on the brink
of tipping forward. He pushed the top forward lightly.
The back rose off the floor, revealing the envelopes
and the money.

Olga quit rather than be arrested.

Solution to **The Case of
Lovely Lana**

Earl had Ginger buy Lovely Lana. He feared someone else might buy it who knew how to care for a pet fish and might beat his Prince in the Pet Fish Club Show.

The vase he gave her had a small opening at the top. He said it would prevent Lovely Lana from jumping out. True, but it would also kill her. It cut down the amount of oxygen in the air from getting to the water. Fish need oxygen to live.

Earl believed Lovely Lana would die in the same amount of time his two killifish had died from lack of oxygen. She'd be dead before the show. A dead fish, he thought, would not be permitted in the show. He goofed.

Lovely Lana died during the show. According to the rule, it could still compete.